BREATHING DARKNESS

MATT BIALER

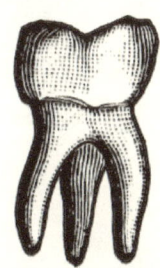

Bizarro Pulp Press books may be ordered through booksellers or by contacting:
Bizarro Pulp Press
www.bizarropulppress.com
or
JournalStone
www.journalstone.com

ISBN: 978-1-947654-99-0 (sc)
ISBN: 978-1-950305-00-1 (ebook)

Bizarro Pulp Press rev. date: March 29, 2019

Printed in the United States of America

Cover Art & Design: Dyer Wilk
Interior Layout: Jess Landry

Edited by Scarlett R. Algee

Seb Doubinsky—
this one is for you

BREATHING DARKNESS

Our son wakes up screaming again

Screaming

We run into the boys' bedroom

Buddy, our border collie,
Pacing and barking

Jared
Ten years old

Max is seven

Both sobbing

Jared

Says he saw the darkness

A man made of darkness

-     How can that be, Jared?
-     It was a nightmare
-     Just a nightmare

It was not a nightmare, Mom

I couldn't sleep

I saw it

Saw the darkness

Saw the darkness move

At first it was a smell

An old smell

Like musky sweat

Buddy is barking at the wall

Something's there

Something's there

I smell something too
Do you smell that, honey?

-     Jared, listen to me
-     You just had a bad nightmare
-     That's all
-     What were you watching on Netflix?
-     We can't let him watch this stuff

A man made of darkness

At first he feels a presence

A presence

The windows are locked

No sign of anyone

Except for that smell

Transformers posters

Aladdin

Giants World Series banner

Out of the corner
Of his eye

Things that move
And vanish

Move
And vanish

A presence

An old smell

Pulls his covers up

A black blob
On the ceiling

That grows

Grows

A shadow

Moves along the wall

Oozing off

Black vapor

It was not a nightmare, Mom

I saw it

Saw the darkness

Saw the darkness move

Can see
A shadow form in the room

A shadow

A man made of darkness

Tall

Wearing a long coat

And hat

A fedora hat

At a strange angle

Clicking sounds

Staring at me

Staring at me

But he has no facial features

No eyes

Can hear it breathe

Breathe

Hear the darkness breathe

He screams

But there is no sound

He screams

I am being marginalized

Marginalized

Under the bus

Out of the loop

404- File Not Found

Rolled

Forced downgrade

I am being marginalized
At work

I'm in the cafeteria
Of the Silicon Valley startup

INTERFAZE:

THE NEXT DIMENSION IN SOCIAL MEDIA

Caesar salads with Roshan

My best friend here

A demo monkey

Late 30s

We're both fathers

He was born in Saudi Arabia

Grew up in New Jersey

I am being marginalized

    -      Are you sure of that, man?

Since the Prince bought us
And his entourage

I'm out of the loop

Is it because they think
My name is a woman's?
The name Pat?

    -      I doubt it

I'm out of the loop

Out of the loop

    -      It's not the Prince
    -      They don't even know who you are

The Saudi prince
Who bought a social media startup

InterFaze

Sounds like everyone is a prince
In Saudi Arabia

    -      There are a lot of them
    -      With different rankings
    -      The Royal Family has some 10,000 members
    -      They like people from here to manage stuff

-        Because they don't like to actually work

InterFaze

I'm cyber security

Best one they have

Best one they have

I don't get e-mails
No new threat warnings
I'm not in meetings

Best one they have

They need me for the Dome

I practically designed it myself

-        You know who it is

-        Do I need to tell you?

-        You know who it is

Le trou de cul

The Asshole

My supervisor
Peter Horgan

Head of our team

Le trou de cul

Nobody likes him

A classic weasel

Called *le trou de cul*
The Asshole
Behind his back

But the Prince
Likes him

Has His Royal Highness
Wrapped around his finger

- He's threatened by you, man
- Everybody knows that

I gotta get out of this place!
I can feel the chill in the air
Brrrr!

- Man I have to deal
- With the ponytails
- They're no fun either
- And besides
- We're going to change social media

We laugh

WE'RE GOING TO CHANGE SOCIAL MEDIA

INTERFAZE

THE NEXT DIMENSION

AI
Artificial Intelligence

AI lab
Here in the building

State of the art
Headed by some guru
From MIT

Image and speech recognition software

To make it super-efficient

Viral videos
You'll find funny

Photos
You'll want to see

Like your friend
In a group photograph

Valuable personal data

InterFaze

With software
Known as FazeLift

Optical character recognition

And computer vision

Using convolution neural networks

The problems of
Invariant visual perception

And how
Deep learning

Can help solve it

Deep learning

Replicated convolutional nets
For recognizing individual objects

Known as
Space displacement neural nets

SDNN

FazeLift

Can pick someone's face
Out of a crowd

Extract the face
From the rest of the scene

Compare to the base
Of stored images

In order for it work
Know how to differentiate

Between a basic face
And the rest of the background

Defines face landmarks
As nodal points

Distance between the eyes
Width of the nose
Depth of the eye socket
Shape of the cheekbones
Length of the jaw

Nodal points measured

Creating a numerical code
Called a faceprint

Representing the face
In the data base

Best one they have

I'm being marginalized

Marginalized

I'm here to keep this technology

Away from the hackers

The Black Hats

Chinese
Russians
North Koreans

Anonymous

Cult of the Dead Cow

LulzSec

Guardians of Peace

Lizard Squad

A new group
Calling itself Smokeless Fire

Cyber security specialist

I'm building the Dome

They need me for the Dome

Keeping cyber crime
At bay

Proficiency in analysis

Forensics and reverse engineering

To monitor and diagnose
Malware events

Make recommendations
For solutions

You can't really try
To protect everything

From everyone

That's not sustainable

No one has the resources

Or capabilities to do that

UNDERSTAND YOUR ATTACKERS

I'm here to protect

At least I thought I was

I'm being marginalized

UNDERSTAND YOUR ATTACKERS

- So you're going to Black Hat, right?

Black Hat Conference in Vegas

No one's told me I'm going

- Man, I'm not even security
- And I'm going
- I'm sure you are

No one told me I'm going

I wasn't in the chain

Not in the chain

- I'm sure you're going

That fuckin asshole

My phone chirps

My wife

-     I got a call from the school today
-     There's concern about Jared

Why is that?

-     He's been very quiet
-     And not attentive
-     Looks tired
-     Lost in his own world

-     They were watching a movie

-     They pulled down the shades

-     He had a meltdown

-     He yelled

-     Wonder if he gets enough sleep

-     They want to know

-     What's going on?

-     What's going on?

3 am
They're both screaming again

Screaming

We run into the boys' bedroom

Buddy pacing and barking

Sobs

I saw it too!

-      You're having nightmares
-      And imagining things

I saw it too!

Says he saw the darkness

A man made of darkness

We both saw it

Saw the darkness

Saw the darkness move

Everything's locked
Windows closed

And there's that smell again

I know that smell

I know it

Buddy barking at the wall

Can we sleep with you tonight?

I pick up Max

I'm scared, Daddy

     -     Jared, I think you're influencing Max

I know that I'm not crazy

We both saw it

We both saw it

     -     It?
     -     What? The bogeyman?

Lying in bed

Trying to fall asleep

Looks up
At the ceiling

A large black mass

Arms and legs

Weird clicking noise

Not humanly possible
To make

Not possible

Oozes down
The wall

Black vapor

Feeling of something
Watching him

Watching him intensely

Something sinister
Dreadful

Shape of a man

Over six feet tall

Stands at the foot
Of the bed

Breathing

No details
Of features

Blacker
Than black

Without really
Having a true color

Except a hint
Of bright blue

Around the outlines

Similar to the color
Of an electric arc

No hat this time

But a cloak

Starts to suffocate him

The pillow

Screams

But no sound

No sound

Max screams

He sees it too

Sees the darkness

Man made of darkness

I'm not sleeping
In here anymore

I'm scared

     –   Ok, guys
     –   It's just a bad nightmare going around

I was awake

It's a ghost

- It's not a ghost

Later

- We have to do something about this
- Now it's both of them

A presence

Did you smell
That weird odor, honey?

- No
- I think Jared should see someone

I think this will pass
These things do

- It's not going to pass

Says he saw the darkness

Saw the darkness move

A man made of darkness

-        Turn out the light!

No, Mommy!
Then it won't go away!

-        Turn out the light!
-        Go to sleep!

2 am

Something in the boy's room

Something

Not friendly

A presence

Standing next
To the left of the bed

The boy closes his eyes

Smells something weird

An old smell

Sweat?

Feels as though

He's blocked

Something
Standing over him

Something

Eyes closed

A presence

Wants to scare him

Inflict terror

Punishment

The boy opens his eyes

He opens his eyes

To see
What the hell it is

There stands
On the left side

Of his bed

A black-cloaked hooded figure

With a hat

Like in black and white movies

Leans over the boy

An old smell

Clicking sounds

Face gray
And snowy

Like a TV screen

When it's all fuzzy

Eyes black

Sunken in snowy face

The boy screams

He screams

But no sound

Instantly pinned
To the bed

Pinned

Punishment

Only body part

He can move

Neck area

Everything else
Locked to the bed

Trying to scream

Scream

Figure leans
Into him

Feels like it's
Shoving an arm down his neck

Choking him

Choking him

Screams

But cannot hear himself

Tears run down
His face

Trying to get up

Look at the attacker

Snowy cloaked face

Leave me alone!

You don't belong here!

Leave me alone!

I am being marginalized

Marginalized

Under the bus

Out of the loop

404- File Not Found

Rolled

Forced downgrade

I am being marginalized
At work

INTERFAZE:

THE NEXT DIMENSION IN SOCIAL MEDIA

I'm out of the loop

Insta-Message
From *le trou de cul*

The Asshole

Never addresses me by name

-        His Royal Highness will be in Vegas

Ok
Am I going too?

Black Hat Conference

Caesars Palace

-         Yes

I did not get the e-mail
I was not on the list

-         The Dome has to be ready
-         No fuck-ups

It's ready
It's ready

-         The Dome has to be ready
-         No fuck-ups

Le trou de cul

The Dome

Cloud website vulnerability
Management platform

Verified security intelligence
Into actionable insights

Through a combination of core products
And strategic partnerships

Complete security
For InterFaze

At a scale
And accuracy
Unmatched
In the industry

Unmatched

The Dome

Hack yourself first approach

Automated and powerful SaaS platform

Sharing details of specific attack vectors

Open XMLAPI integrations

The Dome

It's ready
It's ready

No fuck-ups

Best one they have

Best one they have

Browse Threat Exchange

Forum for sharing information

A bug just announced

An open source program

Called wpa_supplicant

UNDERSTAND YOUR ATTACKERS

Details about notorious virus

Carbanek

Use simple techniques

Like phishing

To trick employees

Into infecting their endpoints

With malware

Study employee behavior
In captured keystrokes and passwords

Steal money
Through fraudulent transactions

UNDERSTAND YOUR ATTACKERS

THE ADVERSARIES DON'T GIVE UP

WHEN THEY'VE BEEN DETECTED

AND KICKED OUT

IF THEY DON'T COME BACK

YOU SHOULD WORRY

BECAUSE IT MEANS

THEY'VE ALREADY TAKEN EVERYTHING

EVERYTHING

-   The Dome has to be ready
-   No fuck-ups

The Dome has to be ready

Le trou de cul

Anonymous peaks in activity
During the weekend

Mostly students

Western people
With normal jobs

Focus on hitting
US and European banks

LulzSec completely inverts
Temporal signature from Anonymous

Peaks on Wednesdays
Peak of internet traffic

I am being marginalized

No fuck-ups

INTERFAZE:

THE NEXT DIMENSION IN SOCIAL MEDIA

With most facial recognition

Even the smallest change in light
Or orientation

Reduces the effectiveness

Can't be matched
To any face in the database

High rate of failure

Not us

Not InterFaze

That's why everyone

Will try to hack us

WE'RE GOING TO CHANGE SOCIAL MEDIA

FazeLift

Skin biometrics

Uniqueness of skin texture

To yield more accurate results

Surface Texture Analysis

A picture taken
Of a patch of skin

Skinprint

Broken into smaller blocks

Using algorithms
To turn the patch

Into mathematical measurable space

Distinguish between lines and pores
And actual skin texture

Can identify the difference
Between identical twins

Identical twins

FazeLift

No fuck-ups

BECAUSE IT MEANS

THEY'VE ALREADY TAKEN EVERYTHING

EVERYTHING

FazeLift

I am being marginalized

Marginalized

My cell phone chirps

Tammy
My wife

     -    I found a doctor
     -    Who specializes in child nightmares

Ok
Maybe we're rushing that

- It's getting worse, Pat
- The school is concerned
- It's affecting his grades

- We have to get to the bottom of this

- We have to

I Google around

Find websites

About Shadow People

Shadow People

Documented encounters

Unknown beings

Shadow People

Sheer panic
And terror they cause

Menacing black forms

Invade bedrooms

Where they stand
And watch sleeping people

Loom over them

Crush them
With suffocating weight

Shadow People

- We have to get the bottom of this
- No fuck-ups

UNDERSTAND YOUR ATTACKERS

Shadow People

Physically attack

Vicious force

Come and go
With unpredictability

Materialize out of thin air

Walk through walls

Emerge from closets

Shadow People

- We have to get to the bottom of this

EVERYTHING

They are for real

Sometimes they appear once

Sometimes for years

Years

Shadow People

    -        What are you reading about, man?

My friend Roshan

I'll tell you at lunch

In the cafeteria
Over burnt burgers

    -        You heard the Prince
    -        Is coming to Vegas?

Yep

    -        I have to rent out
    -        A whole club for him
    -        And the entourage
    -        And if he decides to see a movie
    -        He likes big shoot 'em up action movies
    -        And he likes to watch by himself
    -        What a pain in the ass

    -        So what's that website

    -        You were looking at, man?

I tell him
About the boys

And Shadow People

-       You're serious, aren't you?

I am

-       You don't think it's just nightmares?

Tammy's sure of it

But I'm not

I think it's something else

-       Like?

I don't know

Ghosts

Shadow People

-       Get out of here!
-       Why do you say that, man?

The dog barking like crazy

The strange odor

-       Odor?
-       What kind of odor?

Like musky sweat

But it's not that

- Smell like cumin?

Cumin?

Yes, in fact it does

Cumin

- I went out with this woman
- Who thought Shadow People
- Were chasing her
- Her whole life
- Followed her
- Not all of the time

Really?

Was it a ghost?

- Shadow People are not ghosts

So you do believe this

- Shadow People are Djinn

Djinn?

- Genies to you

Genies? What?

- And I don't mean the one
- In I Dream of Jeannie
- I wish that were the case

Djinn

Ancient race of beings

Masterful shapeshifters

Longstanding grudge

Against human beings

Djinn

Comes from

Arabic verb *janna*

Which means

To hide or conceal

The Hidden Ones

- I know people
- Back home
- Who can help you
- I only know a little

EVERYTHING

UNDERSTAND YOUR ATTACKERS

Shadow People
The Hidden Ones

And Allah created man
From sounding clay
Of black smooth mud

And Allah created the djinn
From the smokeless flame of fire

Smokeless Flame of Fire

And Allah said to the angels

I am going to create man
From sounding clay of mud
Molded into shape

Smokeless Flame of Fire

So when I finish him completely
And breathe into him
The soul which I created for him

Molded into shape

Fall down prostrating yourselves
With him

Fall down

Smokeless Flame of Fire

The angels prostrated themselves
All of them together

All of them

Except one
Except one

Iblis

He refused to be among them

Iblis refused

Smokeless Flame of Fire

Refused to be among them

Allah said

O Iblis
What is your reason
For not being among the prostrated?

Iblis replied

"I am not one to prostrate myself
To a mere human being
Whom you created
From sounding clay of black smooth mud"

Molded into shape

Smokeless Flame of Fire

Allah said

Then get out from here,
For verily, you rajim

Rajim
Outcast

You rajim

UNDERSTAND YOUR ATTACKERS

We take Jared
To see a psychiatrist

THEY'VE ALREADY TAKEN EVERYTHING

Dr. Cindy Jones

OCD

Obsessive-compulsive disorder

Social phobias

Panic attacks

Pounding heart

Shortness of breath

Dizziness

Numbness

Or tingling feeling

-       What do we do?
-       I don't want him medicated

EVERYTHING

-       What do we do?

Cognitive behavior therapy
CBT

Try out new ways
To think and act

In situations
That cause anxiety

And to manage
And deal with stress

Support and guidance

Teach new coping skills

Relaxation techniques

Breathing exercises

UNDERSTAND YOUR ATTACKERS

Learn to identify
And replace negative thinking patterns

Four- to seven-month sessions

One session a week
50 minutes

Understand what the problem is

Develop new strategies
For tackling them

Hands us a book

This will be Jared's diary

Incidents that provoke feelings
Of anxiety and depression

Learn coping skills

Coping skills

And be supportive

Stay with him
Until he falls asleep

Avoid scary television

Have him think
Of a relaxing scene

Like lying on a beach

UNDERSTAND YOUR ATTACKERS

Oozes down
The wall

Black vapor

Shape of a man

Stands at the foot
Of the bed

Breathing

Breathing

A text from Roshan

-      I can get you cheap fare
-      To Riyadh
-      I have some relatives
-      That can help you, man

Oh, I don't know, Roshan
Maybe this will just go away

-      You should do it
-      They might not go away

THEY MIGHT NOT GO AWAY

UNDERSTAND YOUR ATTACKERS

Use your imagination
To fight imaginary fears

Many families
Have found Monster Spray

To be a wonderful way
To help a child cope

With bedtime fears

THEY'VE ALREADY TAKEN EVERYTHING

In the car
On the way home

Text from
Le trou de cul

- His Highness must be pleased
- With the Dome
- State of the art

It is state of the fuckin art
His Highness will be pleased

- Have you utilized TRC?

Threat Research Center

Of course

- And Open XML-API integrations?

Yes, of course

- His Highness is thinking of launching the whole thing
- At the Black Hat

At a convention of hackers? You're kidding me, right?
We could end up on the Wall of Sheep

- Wall of Sheep?

The Wall of Sheep
A public board that displays
The names and partial passwords
That hackers obtained
From unsecured systems

- Well, we're not going to be on that wall
- Not on the wall

Must be pleased

Monster Spray

I'm the best they have

Best they have

FazeLift
Uses three templates

To confirm or identify
The subject vector

Local feature analysis
And surface texture analysis

Vector template very small
And used for rapid searches

Over the entire database

Black vapor

Shape of a man

Stands at the foot
Of the bed

Clicking sounds

Breathing

Breathing

THEY MIGHT NOT GO AWAY

Jared playing a handheld computer game

In the back

Monster Hunter 4

Role of hunter
With a traveling caravan

Explore new lands
And towns along the way

Hundreds of quests
To take on a variety of extraordinary creatures

"Jared, I thought we said
No scary games?"

-    This isn't scary, mom.
-    This is just a game
-    It isn't real

"Just like those creatures you say you see
Aren't real, Jared."

-    Oh, they're real, Mom
-    They're real

"No scary games, Jared."

Sighs
Puts it down

-    Daddy?

Yes, Jared?

-     Didn't you have something
-     That you overcame?

I did
I used to stutter

-     How did you get over it?

Speech therapy
And the cause went away
Over time

-     What was the cause?

Well, there were a bunch of them
You're going to be fine, Jared

I promise

YOU SHOULD DO IT

THEY MIGHT NOT GO AWAY

On the ceiling

That grows

Grows

A shadow

Moves along the wall

Oozing off

Black vapor

It was not a nightmare, Mom

I saw it

Saw the darkness

Saw the darkness move

A man made of darkness

THEY'VE ALREADY TAKEN EVERYTHING

EVERYTHING

At a scale
And accuracy

Unmatched
In the industry

Unmatched

The Dome

The Dome

Time:

Are there any temporal patterns
Regarding cyber attacks?

Are your information assets
More vulnerable at a certain time?

New hacker group Smokeless Fire

Hits Saturday night through Wednesday

Signature red visuals

Screens go red

That night
We stay in the room

With the boys
Until they're asleep

Later
Wakes up screaming

Screaming

His eyes open

Oozes down
The wall

Black vapor

Feeling of something

Watching him

Watching him intensely

Something sinister

Dreadful

A presence

Shape of a man

A man made of darkness

Blacker
Than black

A black coat

Black hat

With a wide brim

No facial features

Except the eyes

Burning red eyes

Clicking sounds

He feels his neck

Being grabbed

Wakes up screaming

But no sound

No sound

Max screams

He sees it too

Sees the darkness

Man made of darkness

Burning red eyes

We run in

Turn on the light

Buddy barking
Like crazy

At the wall

At the wall

Nothing

We see nothing

But I smell it

That old smell

Cumin

A man made of darkness

-      Turn out the light!

No, mommy!
Then it will come back

-      Turn out the light
-      Or I will come in
-      And

Turns out the light

1 am

Something in the boy's room

Something

Not friendly

A presence

Standing to the right
Of the bed

A presence

Tall dark figure
With the hat

No, not you again

No!

Boy closes his eyes

That smell again

Ugly smell

Evil

Standing over him

Something sinister

Inflict terror

Punishment

Feels it

He shoots
Out of bed

Screams

Turns on the lamp

His mother
Rushes into the room

         -        What is it this time?

It came back
That thing

         -        It's nothing
         -        It's just your imagination
         -        You read too many comic books
         -        Now go back to bed

He turns it back on

Squeak
Squeak

What are you doing, Mommy?

-        What do you think
-        I'm doing?

Squeak
Squeak

Don't do that!
Please don't do that!

She unscrews the light bulb

No! No!
Don't do that, Mommy!

Please don't do that!

Leaves him in the darkness

Leaves him

Allah said

Then get out from here,

For verily, you rajim

Rajim

Outcast

You rajim

And Allah continued

And verily, the curse

Shall be upon you

Until the Day of Resurrection

Smokeless Flame of Fire

Iblis said

"O my Lord!

Give me then respite
Till the day

The dead will be resurrected"

Allah said

Then, verily, you are of those reprieved

Till the Day of the Appointed

Smokeless Flame of Fire

Iblis said

"O my Lord, because you misled me,

I shall indeed adorn

The path of error

For mankind on the earth

And I shall mislead them all"

Fire is your abode

To abide in it

Smokeless Flame of Fire

"And I shall mislead them all

From the evil of the whisperer

Who withdraws

Who whispers in the breasts

Of mankind

Of djinn and man

Of djinn and man

And I shall mislead them all"

I arrive
King Khalid International Airport
Riyadh

Roshan's cousin Omar
Picks me up

White tee shirt

Mid-thirties
Sunglasses
Dark hair and beard

Drive through
The poor part of the city

Then the rich part

Large homes
Luxury cars in the driveways

We drive to a house
Surrounded by a wall

A villa

Separate salons
For men and women

Swimming pool in the back

I saw it

Saw the darkness

Saw the darkness move

At first it was a smell

An old smell

Like musky sweat

A man made of darkness

Meet Omar's father
Hani

Ghutrah
Traditional white keffiyeh headdress
And thawb garment

Tell him I work
With his nephew Roshan

He says he knows that

Why am I visiting his country?

Because I want to learn more
About the djinn

Expression changes
From neutral

Eyebrows go up

Concern
Agitation

      -     I didn't know
      -     You westerners knew about them

Most of us don't

Djinn
Comes from
Arabic verb *janna*
Which means
To hide or conceal
The Hidden Ones
Oozes down
The wall

Black vapor

Clicking sounds

Feeling of something
Watching him

Watching him intensely

Something sinister
Dreadful

Shape of a man

Over six feet tall

Stands at the foot
Of the bed

Breathing

No details
Of features

Blacker

Than black

Without really
Having a true color
Breathing

-        This is not made up stuff
-        They are very real
-        And live in my country

Monster Spray

UNDERSTAND YOUR ATTACKERS

Shadow People

Physically attack

Vicious force

Come and go
With unpredictability

Materialize out of thin air

Walk through walls

Emerge from closets

Shadow People

-        We have to get to the bottom of this

EVERYTHING

THEY MIGHT NOT GO AWAY

They are for real

And I shall mislead them all

US military
Has been trying to catch a djinn

For years

Years

Out in the desert

A technological device
That allows them

To pass through solid walls

A different dimension

The Hidden Ones

And I shall mislead them all

Did they catch one?

He shrugs

Smiles

-      Read the Qur'an
-      If you want to know
-      About the djinn
-      Read the Qur'an

Ancient race of beings

Masterful shapeshifters
Longstanding grudge
Against human beings

Molded into shape
Smokeless Flame of Fire

Allah said

Then get out from here,
For verily, you rajim

Rajim
Outcast

You rajim

I saw it

Saw the darkness
Saw the darkness move

A presence

Things that move
And vanish

Move and vanish

A man made of darkness

- This ends our conversation
- About the djinn

Says something in Arabic
To Omar

Tomorrow Omar
Will take me to a mosque

At the edge of the city

Meet a holy man

He knows everything
About the djinn

EVERYTHING

THEY'VE ALREADY TAKEN EVERYTHING

A BLACK BLOB

THEY MIGHT NOT GO AWAY

Next morning
Rundown part of the city

Pull in front of building
Hundreds of years old

Looks like
It was a mosque

Greeted at door

Taken into room

Very old man

Hands trembling

Smoking a water pipe

Omar speaks to him in Arabic

-        Please sit down
-        I will translate
-        Ask any questions
-        About the djinn
-        Nothing more

Get only one response
To each question

No recording devices

Black cloaked hooded figure

With a hat

Like in black and white movies

Leans over the boy

An old smell

Face gray
And snowy

Like a TV screen

When it is all fuzzy

Eyes black

Sunken in snowy face

The boy screams

He screams

But no sound

Allah created
Three intelligent races

Angels
Djinn
And humans

Angels created first
Then the Djinn

Placed here
As stewards and masters

Most loved by Allah

Made of smokeless flame of fire

Long lifespan

Great power

Manipulate matter
And change form

No one knows
How long they live

But they do eventually die

And are answerable to Allah

On the Day of Judgment

Became too powerful

Resentful of human beings

Allah cast them
Into a parallel world

Close to our own

His hand trembles

Trembles

Iblis was
The most powerful of the djinn

He betrayed Allah

Betrayed him

He was angry

Smokeless Flame of Fire

Refused to be among them

Allah said

O Iblis
What is your reason

For not being among the prostrated?

Iblis replied

"I am not one to prostrate myself
To a mere human being
Whom you created
From sounding clay of black smooth mud"

Molded into shape

Smokeless Flame of Fire

Allah said

Then get out from here
For, verily, you rajim

Rajim

Outcast

You rajim

Saw the darkness
Saw the darkness move

A man made of darkness

A call from my wife Tammy

-       When are you coming home?

In a day or two
It's just last-minute stuff
Before the launch

How's Jared?

-       Still the same
-       He's drawing these horrible hooded creatures
-       In the diary

Text from
Le trou de cul

-       We're launching at Black Hat

Great
Let's attract all of the hackers

-       We're not ending up on that goat wall

Goat?

-       Yeah that wall
-       Goat of shame?

You mean the Wall of Sheep

-       Is the Dome ready?

Yes

- His Royal Highness wants to unveil
- His cutting-edge facial recognition technology
- And his great firewall security dome at the same time
- We can't fuck this up

I didn't even know
I was going to Black Hat

I am being marginalized

Marginalized

Under the bus

Rolled

Out of the loop

I'm the best they have

Best they have

Small passenger jet
Lands at Muscat
International Airport

- Do you even know where we are, Pat?

Not really

- We're near the Gulf of Oman

Region called

The Eastern Hajar Mountains

We're going to meet a person

Who will take us to a cave

That, it is said,

A djinn inhabits

A djinn inhabits

Drive south
Major road
Blue water

Breathtaking views
Of mountains

Arrive afternoon

Meals
Drinks

Visit a mosque

Someone overhears us

Tells us not to mess
With the djinn

Not to mess with them

A black blob

On the ceiling

That grows

Grows

A djinn inhabits

A shadow

They are returning to our world
They are returning

THEY MIGHT NOT GO AWAY

THEY'VE ALREADY TAKEN EVERYTHING

The next morning
Quick breakfast

Meet our guide
With his Jeep

Climbing gear
And two 9mm pistols in the back

-        They're for the bandits

In order to get into the cave
Rappel down 300 feet

I used to climb
In college

Cave ten miles south

We park

Hike a mile

Salt flats

Lichens

Succulents

Reach the top of the hill

A large hole
Diameter, ten feet

One of three entrances

Guide speaks in English

    -       Are you ready to go, my friend?

You guys aren't coming?

    -       Oh no, we stay here

Anchor several clamps
In the rocks

Hook the rope
On rappelling harness

Begin my slow descent
Into cave

Halfway down

A red mist

Begins to rise up

Red mist

Rise up

From the darkness
Of the cave

Smoke shadows
Flicker

Think I hear chants

Clicking sounds

Arabic voices

Shadows

Red mist

Stop my descent

Mist a larger form

Growing

Not illuminated by the sun

But glowing

Flickering

Dark shadows

Hear a voice again
English

LEAVE HERE NOW

LEAVE HERE NOW

I see my two companions
Conversing in Arabic

Panicked

They start to run

I'm hanging about
75 feet

Then get out from here,
For verily, you rajim

Rajim
Outcast

Rajim
Outcast

You rajim

Saw the darkness
Saw the darkness move

A man made of darkness

LEAVE HERE NOW

Climb down

See them running
To the vehicle

Get out of my climbing gear

Yell for them

Don't leave me!

Omar says

-      Hurry! It was a djinn!

Run after them

What's going on?

They're praying in Arabic

Climb into the Jeep

-      It was a djinn
-      Telling us to get out of here

And we are
We are

I'm at the Black Hat Conference

Ballroom
Caesars Palace

Thousands of security experts

Electronic locks
On our hotel rooms

May not be secure

Hacked

Stay away from
All WiFi

Turn off your Bluetooth

Try to encrypt
Any information
You must send

Use a VPN

People are watching

Anything can get hacked

Anything

ATMs
Room keys

RFIP cards

Don't be a lamb

Don't be a lamb

We're launching

INTERFAZE
THE NEXT DIMENSION
IN SOCIAL MEDIA

InterFaze

Don't be a lamb

Correlate/normalize
US general interest activity

Per country
Potentially with Internet census data

Hacker teams regularly begin
Work at 8 am

Beijing time

Continue through standard work day

But sometimes persist
Until midnight

Don't be a lamb

A hacker claims
He hacked a United Airlines plane's control system
While in the air

People are watching

Don't be a lamb

Recognize the security industry's
Biggest achievements and failures

The Pwnie Awards

The Oscars of Hacking

People are watching

Award for Epic Fail

Award for Best Song

"Give It Some Salt"

Password breach
In rap form

A party at Omnia Nightclub
In Caesars Palace

Hackers and security suits
Mingle

Pose for pictures
With dancers

Dressed in little more
Than a layer of mud

Bartenders wear black cloaks
Wide-brimmed black hats

Pose for pictures

Another party at
The Cosmopolitan Marque Nightclub

Hackers
Security researchers
Executives

Drink from giant ice luge
Emblazoned with the word
MICROSOFT

9 pm
I'm up in my room

With my laptop

Phone chirps

Roshan

- Hey man
- Why aren't you at the dinner?
- We're at the hottest club
- In the best casino
- That's what the Prince wanted
- At the last minute
- VIP table
- Cost 5 grand in bribes
- Why aren't you here?

I wasn't invited

- I'm sure you're invited

Ask le trou de cul

-     What?

Ask Peter Horgan

Rajim
Outcast

-     Hold on
-     He says it was an oversight
-     You can come

Yeah right
Well, I already ate
And somebody has to guard the fort

Don't be a lamb

People are watching

-     Man, we blew people away
-     The next dimension in social media
-     I'm beginning to believe

INTERFAZE

THE NEXT DIMENSION IN SOCIAL MEDIA

Later that night
I'm half asleep

I saw it
Saw the darkness move

Can see

A shadow form in the room

A shadow

Clicking sounds

Siren on my laptop

A hack attempt

I open it

Don't be a lamb

THEY'VE ALREADY TAKEN EVERYTHING

EVERYTHING

Open it

Clicking sounds

Arabic chants

My screen is red

Siren on my laptop

Red mist

The next day
Jared calls me at the hotel

- Daddy
- Still no sign of them
- Still no sign
- Ever since you came back
- From that trip
- They've been gone

Gone

The launch of InterFaze

A smashing success

And the Dome held

We were not on the Wall of Sheep

The Dome held

Don't be a lamb

INTERFAZE

WE'RE GOING TO CHANGE SOCIAL MEDIA

With software
Known as FazeLift

Optical character recognition

And computer vision

Using convolution neural networks

The problems of
Invariant visual perception

And how
Deep learning

Can help solve it

Deep learning

Replicated convolutional nets
For recognizing individual objects

Known as
Space displacement neural nets

SDNN

FazeLift

Can pick someone's face
Out of a crowd

Extract the face
From the rest of the scene

Compare to base
Of stored images

His Royal Highness
Sends out a memo

Singles out Peter Horgan
For his brilliance and vision
For the future of cyber security

The best in the business

Understands the attackers

He is promoted

Brilliance and vision
In the future of cyber security

Promoted

That night
I'm sleeping

Or at least
I think I am

There's that smell again

That old ugly smell

Clicking sounds

Feeling of something
Watching me

Watching me intensely

Something sinister
Dreadful

Shape of a man

Over six feet tall

Stands at the foot

Of the bed

A man made of darkness

Breathing

No details
Of features

Blacker than black

Just standing there

Breathing

Photo credit: Izzy Lapidus

Matt Bialer is the author of 16 volumes of poetry including
ASCENT and WONDER WEAVERS (Bizarro Pulp Press),
FORMATION (Weirdo Magnet), DISTANT SHORES
(Villipede Publicatons), THE VALLEY OF THE RIGHT
and THIRD EYE OF THE INNER LIGHT (Leaky Boot
Press). His poems have appeared in many print and online
journals, including Retort, Le Zaporogue, Green Mountains
Review, Gobbet, Forklift Ohio and H_NGM_N.

In addition, Matt is an acclaimed black and white street
photographer who has exhibited his work widely. Some of
his images are in the permanent collections of The Brooklyn
Museum, The Museum of the City of New York, and The New
York Public Library. He is also an accomplished watercolor
landscape painter with work in many private collections.

www.ingramcontent.com/pod-product-compliance
Lightning Source LLC
Chambersburg PA
CBHW020632130626
46552CB00003B/1182